TO:
....

FROM:
....

ON THE
OCCASION OF:
....

DATE:
....

You Are What You Eat

and Other Mealtime Hazards

by Serge Bloch

STERLING

New York / London

Library of Congress Cataloging-in-Publication Data

Bloch, Serge.
   You are what you eat and other mealtime hazards / by Serge Bloch.
      p. cm.
   Summary: A boy who does not like trying new foods receives many confusing words of advice in the form of such phrases as
"people need three square meals a day" and "I knew you were a tough cookie."
   ISBN 978-1-4027-7130-9 (hardcover-plc with jacket : alk. paper) [1. Figures of speech–Fiction. 2. Food habits–Fiction.
3. Humorous stories.] I. Title.
   PZ7.B61943Yo 2010
   [E]–dc22

                                                    2009052299

Lot#: 10 9 8 7 6 5 4 3 2 1
08/10

Published by Sterling Publishing Co., Inc.
387 Park Avenue South, New York, NY 10016
Text © 2010 by Sterling Publishing Co., Inc.
Illustrations © 2010 by Serge Bloch
Distributed in Canada by Sterling Publishing
c/o Canadian Manda Group, 165 Dufferin Street
Toronto, Ontario, Canada M6K 3H6
Distributed in the United Kingdom by GMC Distribution Services,
Castle Place, 166 High Street, Lewes, East Sussex, England BN7 1XU
Distributed in Australia by Capricorn Link (Australia) Pty. Ltd.
P.O. Box 704, Windsor, NSW 2756, Australia

The artwork for this book was created using pen and ink drawings with photography.

Printed in China
All rights reserved

Sterling ISBN: 978-1-4027-7130-9

For information about custom editions, special sales, premium and
corporate purchases, please contact Sterling Special Sales Department
at 800-805-5489 or specialsales@sterlingpublishing.com.

Designed by Katrina Damkoehler

My mother always says, "You are what you eat."

So I'm *very* careful about what I put on my plate.

If my dog, Roger, can eat the same thing all the time, why not me?
"Use your noodle!" my mother said.

"People need **three square meals** a day."

Dad said that my goose would be cooked

if I ate macaroni for *every* meal.

Then he told me that I needed to start thinking
outside the box.

Before breakfast, my sister yelled,
"Last one to the table is a **rotten egg!**"

Dad sounds proud when he says that *she* eats like a horse.

My mother says it drives her bananas
to see *me* eat like a bird.

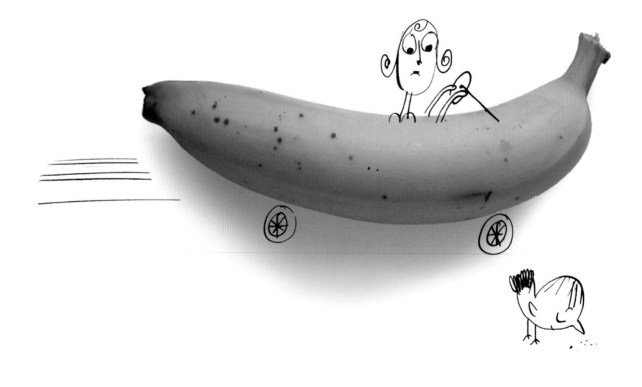

But she also says she's glad I'm not a
couch potato like my dad.

My best friend, Oliver, called to invite me over to his house.
"Don't be late," he said. "The **early bird gets the worm!**"

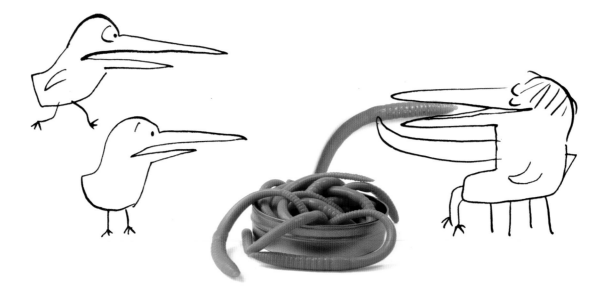

My sister said she wouldn't eat at Oliver's house for
all the tea in China…

...because his mother is a real **health nut**.

Dad told me to take my sister with a grain of salt.

Then he said that I should see the glass as half full, and just enjoy myself.

"You'll be as **cool as a cucumber**," he assured me.

When my mother dropped me off in front of Oliver's house,
she told me not to be nervous,
and said that I was the apple of her eye.

"One *bad apple* spoils the whole barrel,"
my sister muttered from the back seat of the car.

Oliver opened the front door before I could even knock.
He said he could already hear my stomach growling!

I said hello to Oliver's mother and warned her
that I was not very hungry.
She just smiled and said she hoped she could
make me eat my words.

NOT VERY HUNGRY

She asked Oliver to be a **good egg** and set the table.

Then she reminded him not to **eat like a pig**,

especially since he had a guest.

Oliver grinned at me. "We're having something that will really **stick to your ribs**: tofu dogs!"

"Are you all right, dear?" Oliver's mother asked me.

"You look a little green around the gills."

I didn't want to be rude, so I bravely held out my plate.

"I knew you were a tough cookie," said Oliver's mother.

Oliver told me I was as **nutty as a fruitcake** if I didn't love his mother's cooking. So I closed my eyes and took a big bite.

It was delicious!

"Told you so!" said Oliver.

We both asked for seconds. Oliver's mother smiled
and said we were like two peas in a pod.

When Dad came to pick me up, he said I looked like the
cat that swallowed the canary.

My sister asked if I had **chickened out,**

and I surprised her by saying I had eaten even more than Oliver.

My mother said she was as pleased as punch when I tasted a little bit of *everything* she cooked that night.

Why not?
Variety is the spice of life!

ACHOO!